COME BACK, ZACK!

By Trish Holland • Illustrated by Sachiko Yoshikawa

To my son
Goodbye, Zack! Have fun at college! —*T.H.*

 A GOLDEN BOOK • NEW YORK

Text copyright © 2008 by Trish Holland. Illustrations copyright © 2007 by Sachiko Yoshikawa. All rights reserved. Published in the United States by Golden Books, an imprint of Random House Children's Books, a division of Random House, Inc., New York. Golden Books, A Golden Book, A Little Golden Book, the G colophon, and the distinctive gold spine are registered trademarks of Random House, Inc.
Library of Congress Control Number: 2007923684
ISBN: 978-0-375-84269-6
www.goldenbooks.com
www.randomhouse.com/kids
Printed in the United States of America
10 9 8 7 6 5 4 3 2 1
First Random House Edition 2008

Bright, bouncy balls.
Away Zack crawls.

Momma says,
"Come back, Zack!"

Boxes with bows.
Cruising Zack goes.

Daddy says, "Come back, Zack!"

Dandy duck waddles.
Behind, Zack toddles.

Sister says, "Come back, Zack!"

Ice cream in a cup.
Zack climbs up.

Brother says,
"Come back, Zack!"

Perky parrot talks.
Over Zack walks.

Grandma says,
"Come back, Zack!"

Amazing magic trick.
Zack runs quick.

Grandpa says, "Come back, Zack!"

Clowns in a car. Zack pedals far.

Auntie says, "Come back, Zack!"

Hooves whack
and smack.
Along gallops
Zack.

Uncle says,
"Come back, Zack!"